King o' the Cats

told by **Aaron Shepard** illustrated by **Kristin Sorra**

Atheneum Books for Young Readers New York London Toronto Sydney Singapore

For Rowan, Bramble, and Skeeter
—A. S.

For Dennis, the mad storyteller, and Mama, the queen o' the cats
—K. S.

Atheneum Books for Young Readers
An imprint of Simon & Schuster Children's Publishing Division
1230 Avenue of the Americas
New York, New York 10020
Text copyright © 2004 by Aaron Shepard
Illustrations copyright © 2004 by Kristin Sorra
Book design by Abelardo Martínez
The text of this book is set in Lydian.
The illustrations are rendered in oil.
Manufactured in China
First Edition
2 4 6 8 10 9 7 5 3 1
Library of Congress Cataloging-in-Publication Data
Shepard, Aaron.
King o' the cats / Aaron Shepard ; illustrated by Kristin Sorra.—1st ed.
p.   cm.
Summary: A church sexton, known for his wild tales, has three weird encounters with magical cats and can't convince
Father Allen that they really happened, until the priest's cat shows an intense interest.
ISBN 0-689-82082-8
[1. Fairy tales. 2. Folklore—England. 3. Cats—Fiction.]
I. Sorra, Kristin, ill. II. Title.
PZ8.S3425 Ki 2003
[398.2]—dc21   2002005292

ABOUT THE STORY

This is a much expanded retelling of the story told by the great English folklorist Joseph Jacobs in his *More English Fairy Tales* (1894). Other versions are found in Ireland and in continental Europe, where the cats may be replaced by other creatures—even tree spirits or werewolves. The oldest known version features the Greek demigod Pan, as related by Plutarch in the first century A.D. and found in his *Moralia*.

For a reader's theater script of my retelling, plus more about the story, visit my Web site at www.aaronshep.com.

—Aaron Shepard

Young Peter Black was a good man, but everyone said he had one big fault. He loved to tell wild stories.

Peter was the sexton at the Church of St. Thomas the Believer, there in the little town of Tabby-on-Thames. He stayed in the cottage behind the church, right next to Father Allen's house. Many were the jobs he'd held before that, but with his wild stories, he'd managed to lose every one.

Father Allen had warned him. "Peter, this is the last job you're likely to get in this town. If you want to keep it, your wild stories must stop!"

One night Peter couldn't sleep. He tossed and he turned and at last he got up to make himself some tea. But when he glanced out his window, he saw the windows of the church ablaze with light.

"What in the world . . . ?" muttered Peter. "There shouldn't be anyone there this time of night. And how'd they get in, anyway?"

Peter pulled on a coat, crossed the yard, and quietly unlocked the back door. As he crept through the vestry, he heard a sound from the church. Meow, meow.

"Sounds like a cat," murmured Peter. "But I never knew a cat to light a candle."

He peered around the curtain hung at the church entrance, and what he saw made him gasp. There was not *one* cat, but *hundreds* of cats, of every size and coloring. They filled the pews, and all of them sat upright just like people.

On the steps to the altar, a big, black cat— the biggest cat Peter had ever seen—was kneeling with his head bowed. Standing above him with paws upraised was a black cat in bishop's robes, intoning, "Meow, meow . . ."

An altar kitten approached with a velvet pillow on which lay a small, golden crown. The bishop lifted the crown and solemnly placed it on the kneeling cat's head.

The church exploded with cries of *meow, meow!* Peter didn't wait to see more. He raced through the vestry and back to his cottage, where he jumped into bed and stayed trembling under the covers till morning.

Bright and early, Peter was over to see Father Allen. The priest was reading in the conservatory, his black cat, Tom, curled up on his lap.

"Good morning, Peter," said the priest. "What brings you here so early?"

"Father Allen, I came to tell you about something terribly weird in the church last night. I saw these lights and I went over to check, and I heard a *meow*—"

"Meow," said the priest's cat, Tom.

"Yes, just like that," said Peter. "And when I looked, there were hundreds of cats in the church. And there was this one big, black cat, and he was kneeling in front, and their bishop was crowning him. . . ."

Father Allen was looking at him sternly. "Peter, do you remember what I told you about wild stories?"

"Of course I do, Father."

"Then let's have no more of this, all right?"

"But, Father—"

"Listen, Peter, I have an errand for you. Will you walk over to Brambleton today and deliver a message to Father Rowan?"

Peter would and Peter did. But he didn't get to it till late afternoon, and by the time he started home, it was already dusk. He decided to take a shortcut cross-country.

He was halfway through a meadow and up to a stand of trees when he heard a commotion. From beyond the meadow came the barking of a dog and a chorus of *meow, meow.*

"Is it those cats again?" said Peter in alarm, ducking behind a tree.

An Irish setter raced into the meadow, barking for all it was worth. Right behind were a dozen cats with bows and arrows, riding—yes, *riding*—on the backs of bridled foxes. The big, black cat at their head was wearing a golden crown.

At first Peter thought the setter was leading the cats on the trail of their quarry. Then he realized, *No, they're hunting the dog!*

As the cat with the crown rode by a large rock, his fox tripped and stumbled, and the cat went flying. He struck his head on the rock and lay still.

The other cats gave up the chase and crowded anxiously around him. Then with loud, mournful cries of *meow, meow,* they laid him over the back of his fox and returned the way they had come.

Peter stood shaking till they were out of sight, then nipped off home as fast as his wobbly legs would bear him. He found Father Allen at supper, with his cat, Tom, nibbling from a dish by the table.

"Father, it's about those cats. I was crossing a meadow, and I heard a dog barking and all these cats crying *meow*—"

"*Meow*," said Tom.

"Yes, just like that," said Peter. "And then the cats came riding into the meadow on foxes, all of them chasing this dog, but then the cat with the crown fell off and hit his head and . . . and . . . and . . . Father, why's Tom staring at me like that?"

Father Allen put down his fork. "Peter, I've warned you often enough about your wild stories. Now, if you come to me talking like this again, I'm going to have to let you go. Do you understand?"

"But, Father, it's no story. I swear it!"

"That's *enough*, Peter! Now, I'm sorry to ask you so late, but I have another chore for you. Mrs. Pennyweather has passed on suddenly, and tomorrow's the funeral. I need you to dig her grave—tonight."

So it was that Peter was digging in the graveyard by the light of the full moon. It was hard work, and he had to keep resting, and it wasn't till right around midnight that he finished.

Just as he was about to climb out, he heard a distant *meow*, then again, *meow*, and again, *meow*.

"It's the cats!" declared Peter. He scrunched down in the grave, then carefully peered over the edge.

Coming across the graveyard was the black bishop cat, and behind him were six more black cats, carrying on their shoulders a small coffin. The box was covered with a pall of black velvet, and sitting on top was the golden crown that Peter had seen twice before.

The cats walked slowly and solemnly, and at every third step cried *meow*. Their path went right by the grave where Peter hid, and when they were but a few feet away, the bishop held up a paw for a halt. Then he turned and stared straight at Peter and *spoke*.

"Tell Tom Tildrum . . . that Tim Toldrum's . . . *dead*."

Then he lowered his paw, and the cats walked on, and at every third step cried *meow*.

Well, Peter scrambled out of that grave and bolted for Father Allen's.

He pounded on the door, shouting "Father! Father! Let me in!"

At last the door opened and Father Allen stood there sleepily in his nightgown. "Peter, what's going on?"

"Let me in, Father, please, and I'll tell you."

Father Allen led him into the library, where Tom yawned and stretched on his cat bed. The priest lit a lamp.

"Now, what's this all about, Peter?"

"Father, you've got to believe me. I was out digging Mrs. Penny-weather's grave when I heard a *meow*—"

"*Meow*," said Tom.

"Yes, just like that," said Peter. "And I looked and saw seven black cats, and one was the bishop, and the others were carrying a coffin with a crown, and they came right up next to me, and the bishop stopped them and stared at me just like Tom there and . . . and . . . and . . . Father, why's Tom staring at me like that?"

"Peter—" began the priest.

"But, Father, I tell you, he *spoke* to me! And he gave me a message. I'm to tell Tom Tildrum that Tim Toldrum's dead. But how can I tell Tom Tildrum that Tim Toldrum's dead when I don't know who Tom Tildrum *is*?"

"Peter, this is the last straw. I've warned you again and again—"

"Father! Look at Tom! Look at Tom!"

Tom was swaying, and Tom was swelling, and Tom was standing on his two hind legs, and then Tom *spoke*.

"What? Tim Toldrum dead? Then I'm the King o' the Cats!"

Tom leaped toward the fireplace, and with a single *meow*, he bounded up the chimney and was gone.

Never to be seen again.

Of course, after that, there was no more talk of Peter losing his job. But as for Father Allen . . .

Well, Father Allen was a good man, but everyone said he had one big fault. He loved to tell wild stories—about Tom, the King o' the Cats.